Text and illustrations
by Hanne Türk
translated
by Oliver Gadsby

Neugebauer Press

HIERONYMUS

In the middle of Africa where the sun shines hottest and the jungle is thickest, lives Hieronymus our chameleon.

Hieronymus is not very big – in fact he's not much longer than your foot. But he sits alone high up in the trees, and he's hardly ever afraid. For Hieronymus has everything you need for living deep in the jungle.
With his long curling tail and his clasping feet, he can hold on tight wherever he goes.
And the things he can do with his eyes!
Or with his tongue!
Or with the colour of his skin!
You'll see: he does the most amazing things.

Shh! We must be very quiet, or we'll disturb Hieronymus.
He likes being on his own, you see. In fact, he prefers it that way.

This morning everything is grey. Even Hieronymus is grey.
"Oh dear, all this grey everywhere!" he sighs. With his right
eye he looks up at the grey sky. And with his left eye he looks
down at the grey pool beneath him. (For he can look at both
things at once, just by turning his eyes round.)

And then Hieronymus notices something else in the pool:
a grey chameleon, looking up at him.
"Well I never!" he thinks. "There's another chameleon sitting in
the water that looks just like me. And it's just as grey as I am.
I wonder if I should say hello?"
Hieronymus waits, but nothing happens…
"Oh well, here goes," thinks Hieronymus – he says "Hello!",
and then waits for an answer.

BOOOMMM!

Was **that** the answer?

Hieronymus is suddenly afraid, and he trembles all over.

Another flash bursts through the sky over the jungle: a terrible, blinding flash. And then again: BOOOMMM!

At last Hieronymus realises that it's a storm. What should he do?

"Just wait", Hieronymus decides. "In a storm you should just wait, and not be afraid."

But it's easy to say that. How can a little chameleon not be afraid in such a terrible storm, in the middle of a jungle? Hieronymus wonders how the other chameleon down in the pool is feeling. He looks down, cautiously.

"Good Heavens!" thinks Hieronymus. "He doesn't look at all well. He's gone black! He **must** be scared".

The storm is over.
With trembling legs, Hieronymus climbs down from his tree.
He wants to meet the other chameleon, but where can he be?
"Oh, he must be in the pool," murmurs Hieronymus, creeping
carefully towards it. And there **is** something hiding there.
"Pleased to meet you; I'm called Hieronymus," says Hieronymus,
leaning forward to shake hands with the chameleon in the pool.
But all he feels is the water. Brr! What a shock that was!
"That's odd!" he thinks. "And he looks just like me – except that
he's black all over."
Hieronymus sits by the pool, feeling very puzzled. Then at last
he realizes: "Oh – I've got it all wrong! That's **me** in the water –
it's just my reflection! What a stupid Hieronymus I was!"
(And he also realises why his reflection is black: chameleons
turn black when they're afraid!)

Hieronymus climbs back on to his branch and settles down to think for a while. He tries to sort things out in his mind:
"So, when I'm afraid my skin turns black. I wonder what happens when I calm down again?"
But in the middle of these thoughts, his eyelids close. First the left one, and then the right. (It's warm and peaceful in the sun, and Hieronymus has fallen asleep.)
But what on earth is happening now?
His skin's turning yellow!
What a surprise Hieronymus will get when he wakes up!

"I must be seeing things," he mumbles as he wakes from a very deep sleep, rubbing his eyes. "All of a sudden I've gone yellow!"
"Amazing!" he mutters. "I can be grey, or black, or yellow. Perhaps, if I waited long enough, I could be red or blue!"

Just then a passing fly attracts his attention.
"Hmmm, I like the look of that one!"

Slurrp! His tongue shoots out of his mouth, and the fly is gone:
caught and eaten.

What an extraordinary tongue a chameleon has!
It's as long as Hieronymus' body, as springy as an elastic band,
and as sticky as glue. Hieronymus just has to sit there and wait
for his dinner to fly by.
"It's not as easy as it looks, you know," thinks Hieronymus.
"You have to keep a good look-out and aim precisely,
or you miss your meal."
Hieronymus is very proud of his tongue.
But it annoys him that he is still yellow.
Then he has a new idea . . .

"Should I? – or shouldn't I?" he wonders.

 He is soon so excited that he rushes up and down his perch.
"I'd so love to be red. But that means climbing down again and
 splashing about in the red sand-pit."

And so he climbs down. He can remember exactly where the
 sand-pit is, for it was there that he burst out of his egg
 last August.

The red sand is still damp from the rain, which makes it even
 more fun. The sand soon turns Hieronymus quite red. He even
 does a somersault to make sure he is red from top to toe –
 from the tip of his teeth to the end of his tail.

"I'm so red, so very very red!" he sings
"And you can't get redder than this!"

On the way back, Hieronymus goes down to the pool.
He wants to have a look in his water-mirror.

"I bet I look marvellous – just marvellous!" he giggles, and his heart beats with excitement. "I'll see myself in the mirror and prove that I'm the reddest Hieronymus there ever was!" He's in such a hurry to get to the pool that he doesn't notice that the sand is trickling off his body. First one grain, then another, and then more and more – and here he is by the water shaking his head in disbelief. "Well, how peculiar!" he cries. "I'm not red at all. I'm orange – as orange as an orange but with yellow spots!"

"Oh, I know," says Hieronymus. "Yellow and red make orange. That's what happened. But I couldn't be expected to know **that** straight away."

At last all the last bits of sand have slid off his skin.
"Yellow!" curses Hieronymus. "I'm yellow again.
Yellow is all very well for a lemon,
but it doesn't look very good on a chameleon!"
"If only I were at least blue," he sighs. "As blue as my friend the
humming-bird. Or as blue as the sky. Or as blue as . . . as . . .
as those bilberries."
"Bilberries – bilberries . . ." he thinks.
"Yes, what a fantastic idea!"

He almost tumbles out of the tree
in his hurry to get to the bilberry-bush.
Splatt! There goes the first berry. Splatt! – and the next. The
bilberry juice splashes everywhere. Another berry for his head –
one for his back, and then another. Hieronymus looks as though
he has fallen into a pan full of bilberry jam.
And he is just as sticky, too.
"Doesn't matter!" he says. "Doesn't matter at all, even if I do get
all sticky. I **love** blue!"

Just then, a parrot swoops past.

"What's this?" he thinks. "A leaf with feet?"
Full of curiosity, he flies nearer.
"Oh, it's Hieronymus," he cries, and shakes his head in
amazement. "Hello, green Hieronymus!"
"The parrot can't be talking to me. After all, I'm blue." – and
Hieronymus looks down at his feet.
"Ooh, he's right, I'm green! What's happened now?"
Then he thinks carefully. "Ah, the blue has run, and the yellow
is showing through. **Yellow** and **blue** make **green**.
That's why I'm green!"

It's been a tiring day for Hieronymus in the African jungle. But it's been worth it: he has learnt a lot. Before long, the evening rain is pouring down.

"Ah, that feels good," he thinks, shutting his eyes – first the right one, and then the left. "The rain will wash off the blue juice, and I will be clean and yellow again when I go to sleep. Anyway, yellow isn't such a bad colour after all. Hieronymus lets out another deep yawn.

He's tired and happy.

Shh! We must be very quiet again.

Hieronymus is asleep – where the jungle is thickest and the night is darkest. We don't want to wake him.
He's dreaming of a big tree covered with coloured leaves.
Perhaps he's dreaming of mixing a red leaf with a blue leaf.
And in his dream, Hieronymus knows exactly what colour you get if you mix red and blue.

Of course, we've all known that for a long time, haven't we?

Copyright © 1981, Verlag Neugebauer Press, Salzburg, Austria
Original title: Hieronymus
Copyright © 1981, English text, Neugebauer Press Publishing Ltd.
Published in Great Britain by
NEUGEBAUER PRESS PUBLISHING LTD., London.

ISBN 0 907234 06 2

Printed in Austria